For Janet and my parents. T.O'B.
For Christopher and Harriet. M.G.

First published in 1990
Text copyright © Margaret Greaves, 1990
Illustrations copyright © Teresa O'Brien, 1990
All rights reserved

Printed in Italy
for J.M. Dent & Sons Ltd
91 Clapham High Street
London SW4 7TA

British Library Cataloguing in Publication Data
Greaves, Margaret
Henry's wild morning.
I. Title II. O'Brien, Teresa
823'.914 [J]
ISBN 0-460-88018-7

The illustrations for this book were prepared
using pen and ink and water-colour.

HENRY'S WILD MORNING

MORNING

Margaret Greaves

Illustrated by Teresa O'Brien

J. M. Dent & Sons Ltd
London

Henry was the smallest kitten in the litter, and the only tabby.
His bigger brother Joseph and his sisters Dizzy and Tizzy
sometimes teased him because he was so little.

As they all grew bigger the basket seemed smaller, and Henry
was always the one who got squashed. But he didn't mind.
He was a very cheerful kitten.

One morning he woke up feeling very big and wild. He nipped his brother's tail.

"I'm a tiger," he said. "A big fierce tiger. You can't be a tiger. You've got no stripes."

"Don't show off," said Joseph, chewing Henry's ear.

But Henry pranced into the kitchen and ate his breakfast in a very tigerish sort of way.

Then he jumped onto the kitchen table.

Someone had unpacked a shopping basket there. He found several tins and interesting packets and a big ball of string. He patted the string and it moved.

"Ho!" said Henry. "Tigers fight things!"

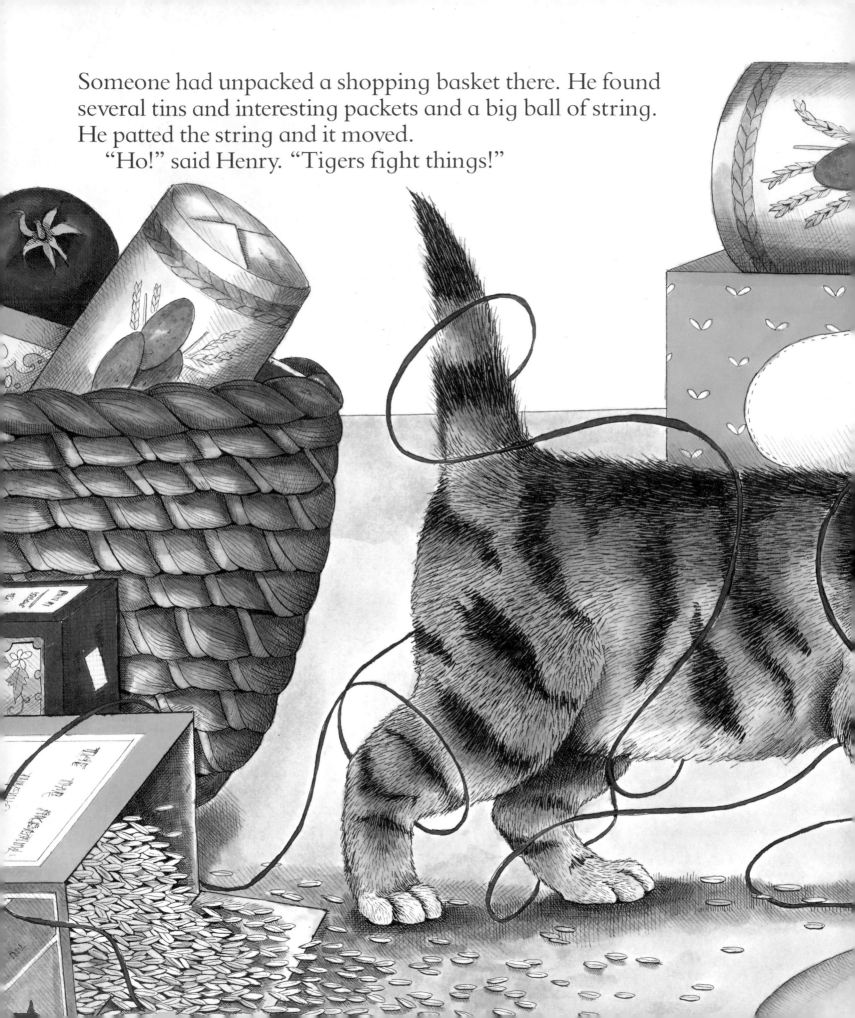

He had a very exciting fight with the ball of string until he knocked over two of the tins. They rolled off the table and across the floor. CRASH, rumble, rumble, BUMP.

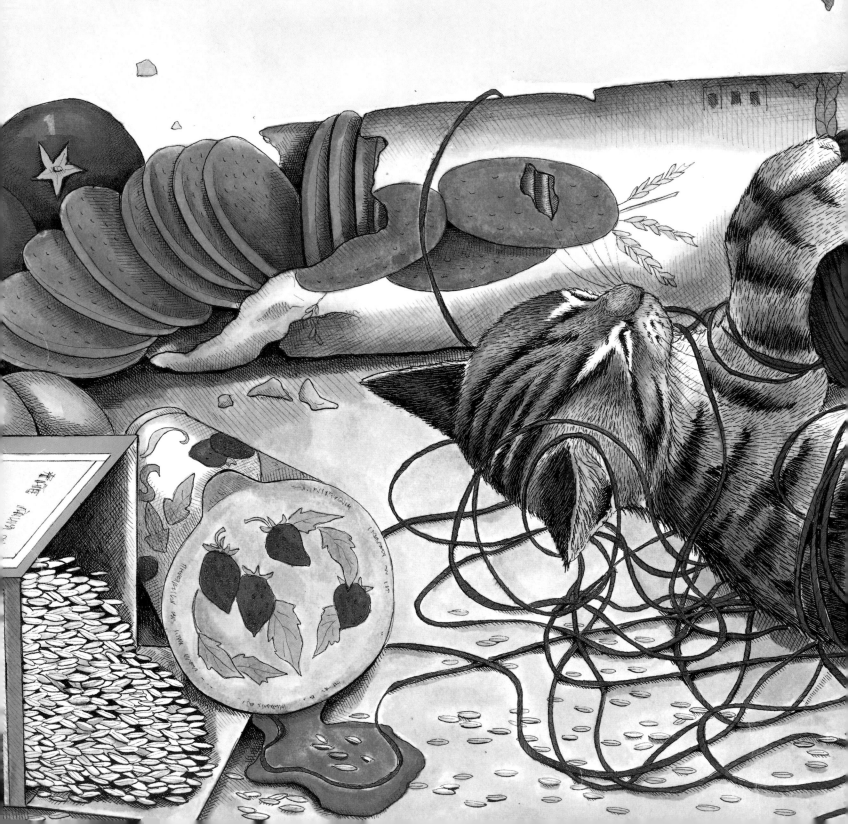

Henry was so scared that he rushed out into the garden. Jasper, the dog next door, pushed his nose through the fence.

"Good morning, little Henry. What are you so scared of?"

"I'm not scared," hissed the kitten, "and I'm not little Henry. I'm a big, fierce, prowling tiger."

He arched his back at Jasper and walked off under some bushes in a prowling sort of way. From there he could see two sparrows pecking on the grass.

He bounced at them, but the sparrows flew up onto the lowest branch of a tree. They perched there, giggling.

"You can't catch us," cheeped one of them.

"You're only a kitten," cheeped the other.

"No, I'm not," said Henry. "I'm a big, fierce, hunting tiger!"

He started to scrabble
up the tree. But the
sparrows flew up to
another branch. Henry
climbed after them,
feeling big and brave.
He had never been so
high before.

He was nearly there when the sparrows flew almost to the top of the tree. They flirted their wings and chirped at him noisily.

"You can't climb this high. You're too small."

"No, I'm not," said Henry. "I'm a big, fierce tiger."

He went on climbing. But when he was very close, the sparrows giggled at him and flew down to the grass again.

Henry looked down at them. Suddenly he saw that the ground was very, very far away. And his branch was thin and wobbly. And he quite forgot about being a tiger.

"Help! Help!" he mewed. "I'm stuck! I'm slipping! Oh help!"

His mother heard him and ran to the bottom of the tree.
"You silly little kitten!" she said. "Now listen. Cats
can't climb down backwards. You must turn round."
"Can't," wailed Henry.

Joseph, Dizzy and Tizzy came out to see what was happening.

"Oooh!" squeaked his sisters. "Fancy getting up there! You are brave, Henry."

That made him feel better, but he still couldn't turn round.

"It's easy," said Joseph (who had never climbed so high). "Move your left front paw to the left, and your right back paw to the right."

Henry nervously moved one paw, then stopped to think. Which was his right paw and which was his left? He never could remember.

"And don't look down," warned his mother. "Henry, DON'T LOOK DOWN!"

She was too late. Henry had already looked down and it made him feel quite dizzy. He was in a terrible muddle about his paws.

Swish! Rustle, crackle, plop!
He had lost his balance and
came falling through the
branches in a shower of leaves
and twigs.

The others rushed to see if he was hurt, but Henry scrambled up and shook himself.

"Did you see?" he squeaked. "I climbed ever so high. Higher than Joseph has, didn't I? I'm a big, fierce tiger."

He was so excited that he tried to scrabble up the tree again.

But his mother grabbed him firmly by the scruff of his neck. "You're NOT a big fierce tiger," she said, shaking him gently, "and you're going straight to your basket."

Henry was quite glad to snuggle down.
Being a tiger was very tiring.

"But I did climb ever so high, didn't I?" he said to his mother.
"Yes, you did, dear," said his mother kindly.

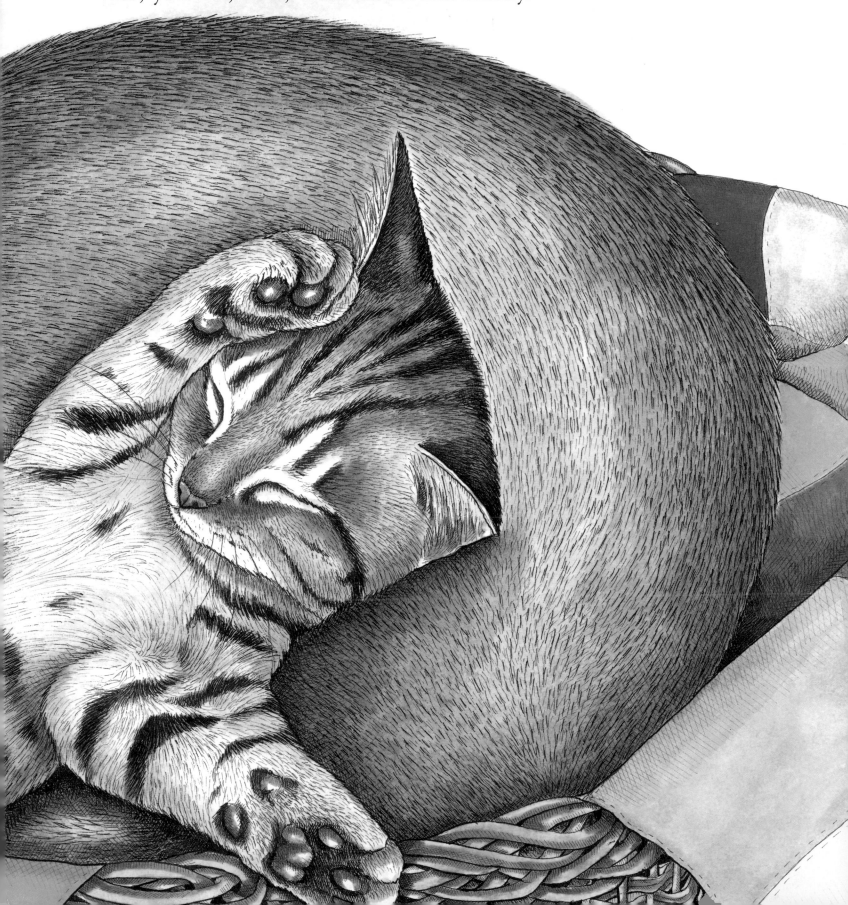

Henry didn't hear her. He was fast asleep.
But in his dreams he was the biggest and
fiercest tiger in the jungle.